Percy the Mailman

A rhyming story
in a familiar setting

This edition first published in 2009
by Sea-to-Sea Publications
Distributed by Black Rabbit Books
P.O. Box 3263
Mankato, Minnesota 56002

Text © Sue Graves 2005, 2009
Illustration © Mike Phillips 2005

Printed in China

A CIP catalog record for this book is
available from the Library of Congress.

ISBN 978-1-59771-161-6

9 8 7 6 5 4 3 2 1

Published by arrangement with the
Watts Publishing Group Ltd, London.

Series Editor: Jackie Hamley
Series Advisors: Dr. Linda Gambrell,
Dr. Barrie Wade, Dr. Hilary Minns
Series Designer: Peter Scoulding

Percy the Mailman

Written by
Sue Graves

Illustrated by
Mike Phillips

SEA-TO-SEA
Mankato Collingwood London

Sue Graves

"I love waiting to see what letters the mailman will bring me. Best of all, I like letters from my friends and invitations to parties!"

Mike Phillips

"I live in Devon, England with my family. I love illustrating all kinds of books, from the shed at the bottom of my garden!"

Percy was a mailman.

He rode a mailman's bike.

6

He delivered lots of letters
To Bernie, Tom, and Mike.

There were letters for Miss Holly,

11

And birthday cards for Sam,

A parcel for Aunt Betty,

And a package for Miss Lamb.

The school got lots of letters.

Percy took them in a sack.

There were cards and
notes and messages,
All bundled in a pack.

"You're lucky getting letters,"
Said Percy looking sad.

"I've never had a letter!
Just a card would make me glad."

"Poor Percy!" said the children
As into school they ran.

Poor Percy!

But Teacher gave a little smile.

She had a clever plan!

Next morning, very early,

Someone knocked on Percy's door.

Rat-a-tat-tat!

Then whizzing through
the letter box,
A letter hit the floor!

Percy tore the letter open.

It said: "We think you're great!

"So open up the door ...

We're waiting at the gate!"

Notes for parents and teachers

READING CORNER has been structured to provide maximum support for new readers. The stories may be used by adults for sharing with young children. Primarily, however, the stories are designed for newly independent readers, whether they are reading these books in bed at night, or in the reading corner at school or in the library.

Starting to read alone can be a daunting prospect. **READING CORNER** helps by providing visual support and repeating words and phrases, while making reading enjoyable. These books will develop confidence in the new reader, and encourage a love of reading that will last a lifetime!

If you are reading this book with a child, here are a few tips:

1. Make reading fun! Choose a time to read when you and the child are relaxed and have time to share the story.

2. Encourage children to reread the story, and to retell the story in their own words, using the illustrations to remind them what has happened.

3. Give praise! Remember that small mistakes need not always be corrected.

READING CORNER covers three grades of early reading ability, with three levels at each grade. Each level has a certain number of words per story, indicated by the number of bars on the spine of the book, to allow you to choose the right book for a young reader:

GRADE 1	GRADE 2	GRADE 3
50 words	130 words	250 words
70 words	160 words	350 words
100 words	200 words	450 words